Since ancient times, people have been inventing different ways of getting around. There are things that travel across land, through water and up in the air.

In this book, there are exactly 1000 vehicles, from folding bicycles and horse-drawn carriages to spacecraft that are exploring our solar system and beyond.

The pictures are not drawn to scale. For example, the ships on page 13 are actually 70 times bigger than the cars on page 9.

Every picture is labelled with its name, and there's a list of all the names at the back of the book.

從 古至今，人類一直發明許多不同類型的交通工具，上天下海，一應俱全。

本書含1000種交通工具，包括摺疊式自行車、馬車、探索太陽系的太空船及更多的載人工具。

書內插圖不按比例繪畫，例如第13頁的船，其實比第9頁的汽車大70倍。

插圖下方標示交通工具之名稱，詞彙表列出書內所有交通工具的英漢名稱。

1000
THINGS THAT GO
兒童英漢詞彙大書
交通工具1000詞

Illustrated by Gabriele Antonini

Researched and edited by Rachel Wilkie and Hannah Wood
Designed by Matt Durber

Expert advice

Alan Barnes, Alexi Holden-Crowther, Andrew Gaved, Anthony Coulls, Ben Holden-Crowther, Brian Voakes, Colin Jarman, David Cousins, David Coxon, David Willey, Doug Hilton, Elfan Ap Rees, James Wilkie, John Robinson, Neil Johnson-Symington, Nicholas Leach, Richard Thompson, Sam Collins, Stephen Courtney, Steve Fowler

商務印書館

Contents 目錄

In the city
Page 5
城市

Racing
Page 10
比賽

Sailing boats
Page 14
帆船

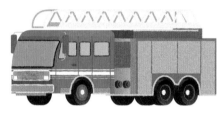

Emergency vehicles
Page 6
緊急救援工具

Motorbikes
Page 11
摩托車

In the water
Page 15
水面或水底

At the airport
Page 7
機場

Famous ships
Page 11
著名的船

In the sky
Page 16
天空

On holiday
Page 8
度假

Historic ships
Page 12
具歷史意義的船

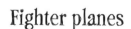

Fighter planes
Page 17
戰鬥機

Lots of cars
Page 9
各式汽車

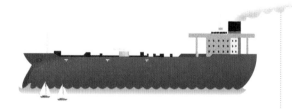

Big ships
Page 13
大型船艦

Tanks and armoured vehicles Page 18
坦克及裝甲車

3

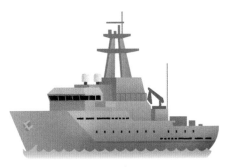

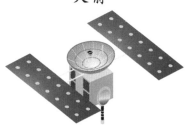

In the city 城市

London
Underground train
倫敦地鐵

Boda-boda
bicycle
東非的一種自行車

Bendy bus
雙節巴士

Black cab
倫敦計程車

Delivery van
小型送貨車

School bus
校車

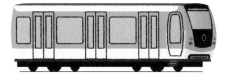
Paris Metro train
巴黎地鐵

Post van
郵車

Powered
wheelchair
電動輪椅

Cyclo
後腳踏人力車

Moped
輕便摩托車

Van
廂形貨車

Electric
bicycle
電動自行車

New York Subway train
紐約地鐵

Double-decker
bus
雙層巴士

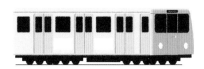
Berlin U-Bahn train
柏林地鐵

Matatu
肯亞的小巴

Hong Kong Mass
Transit Railway train
港鐵

Mobility
scooter
電動代步車

Bike-share
bicycle
公共自行車

Trisikad taxi
前腳踏人力車

Thai tuk-tuk
泰國嘟嘟車

Waste disposal
truck
垃圾車

Tokyo Metro train
東京地下鐵

Folding bicycle
摺疊自行車

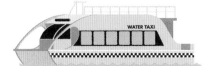
Water taxi
水上計程車

Yellow taxi
黃頂計程車

Pizza delivery
scooter
薄餅店外賣摩托

Motor scooter
"綿羊仔"摩托踏板車

Indian auto-
rickshaw
印度機動三輪車

Streetcar
電車

Utility bicycle
實用自行車

Minibus
小巴

Street sweeper
洗街車

Moscow Metro train
莫斯科地鐵

Emergency vehicles 緊急救援工具

Fire truck
消防車

Emergency doctor car
緊急醫生車

Blood service car
血液運送車

Ambulance
救護車

Cave rescue vehicle
洞穴拯救車

Lifeboat
救生船

Police dog van
警犬車

Police van
警車

Search and rescue vehicle
搜索拯救車

Lifeguard patrol vehicle
巡邏救生車

Mountain rescue vehicle
攀山拯救車

Veterinary ambulance
獸醫救護車

Bomb disposal vehicle
拆彈車

All-terrain fire vehicle
全地形消防車

Rapid response ambulance car
快速應變急救車

Fire motorbike
消防摩托車

Ambulance motorbike
救護摩托車

Police motorbike
警察摩托車

Police bicycle
警察自行車

Traffic police car
交通警車

Mines rescue vehicle
礦井拯救車

Motorsport rescue car
賽車運動拯救車

Police patrol car
巡邏警車

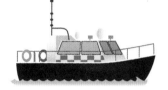
Police boat
水警船

Fire-fighting helicopter
消防直升機

Surf rescue boat
衝浪拯救船

Lifeguard boat
救生員船

Coastguard boat
海岸警衛隊船

Coastguard helicopter
海岸警衛隊直升機

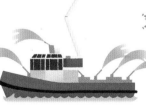
Fire boat
消防船

Rescue helicopter
救援直升機

Air ambulance
空中救護車

Police helicopter
警察直升機

Fire-fighting water bomber
消防水彈飛機

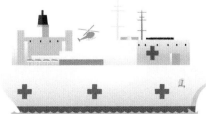
Hospital ship
醫療船

Emergency rescue ship
緊急救援船

Armoured special forces vehicle
特種部隊裝甲車

Submarine rescue vehicle
潛水拯救車

At the airport 機場

Security vehicle
保安車

Baggage truck
行李運送車

'Follow me' truck
飛機引導車

Double-deck plane
雙層飛機

De-icing truck
除雪車

Airside transfer bus
停機坪巴士

Airport caddy
機場內接駁車

Front-entry cargo plane
前端裝卸貨機

Rear-entry cargo plane
後端裝卸貨機

Airport shuttle train
機場接駁列車

Airport maintenance truck
機場保養車

Customs vehicle
海關車

Four-engined jet plane
四引擎噴射機

Runway sweeper
跑道清潔車

Airport fire appliance
機場消防車

Mobile baggage conveyor
行李輸送車

Cargo loader
貨物裝卸車

Shuttle bus
穿梭巴士

Regional jet
區域航線客機

Turboprop plane
渦輪螺旋槳式飛機

Corporate jet
商務噴射機

Three-engined jet plane
三引擎噴射機

Twin-piston aircraft
雙活塞式飛機

Jumbo jet
廣體飛機

Twin-engined plane
雙引擎飛機

Airport fuel truck
飛機加油車

Lavatory service vehicle
污水車

Air start unit
氣源車

Aircraft tug
飛機拖把

Jetliner
噴射客機

Aircraft catering truck
飛機航膳餐車

Ground power unit
電源車

Boarding stair truck
客梯車

Passenger lift
旅客登機車

Side-entry cargo plane
側方裝卸貨機

On holiday 度假

Canal boat
運河船

Hire car
租用車

Caravan
露營拖車

Camper van
小型露營車

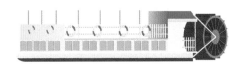
Riverboat
內河客船

Swan boat
天鵝船

Speedboat
快艇

Inflatable ringo
充氣救生圈

Wakeboard
寬板滑水板

Jet ski
小型噴射快艇

Water ski boat
滑水船

Water skis
滑水板

Floating restaurant
水上餐廳

Paddle steamer
槳輪蒸汽船

Golf buggy
高爾夫球車

Motorhome
露營車

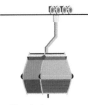
Cable car
纜車

Luxury yacht
豪華遊艇

Chair lift
登山吊椅

Cruise ship
遊輪

Hydrofoil scooter
水上自行車

Ice cream van
雪糕車

Sight-seeing helicopter
觀光直升機

Open-top tour bus
開篷觀光巴士

Trackless train
無軌列車

Safari vehicle
野生動物觀賞車

Tour coach
觀光巴士

Segway PT
賽格威電力雙輪車

Skis
滑雪板

Roller skates
輪式溜冰鞋

Rollerblades
直排輪鞋

Surfboard
衝浪板

Snowboard
滑雪板

Windsurfing board
滑浪風帆板

Ice skates
溜冰鞋

Rollercoaster train
過山車

Rubber dinghy
橡皮艇

Banana boat
香蕉船

Pedalo
腳踏輪槳船

Zip-line
溜索

Bumper car
碰碰車

Lots of cars 各式汽車

Kei car
輕型車

Bubble car
泡泡車

Hardtop
硬頂小汽車

3-door hatchback
三門掀背車

Classic car
老爺車

Hybrid car
混合動力車

Sports car
跑車

Muscle car
肌肉車

Multi-purpose
vehicle
多用途車

City car
城市車

Gullwing car
鷗翼車

Kit car
組件車

Solar car
太陽能汽車

Supercar
超級跑車

Cabriolet
敞篷車

Four-wheel drive
四驅車

Coupé
雙門小轎車

Electric car
電動車

5-door
hatchback
五門掀背車

Le Mans classic car
利曼老爺車

Crossover
跨界休旅車

Estate car
旅行車

Roadster
單排座敞篷小客車

Microcar
迷你車

Hot hatch
小型跑車

Classic cabriolet
老爺敞篷車

Luxury car
豪華汽車

Track day car
賽道日用車

Saloon car
轎車

Three-wheeler
三輪汽車

Classic limousine
經典加長型轎車

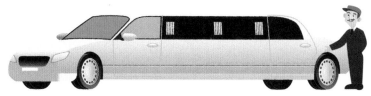
Stretch limousine
加長型轎車

Racing 比賽

Hydroplane
水上飛機

Dragster motorbike
短程競速摩托車

Dragster
直線競速賽車

Top fuel dragster
頂級直線競速賽車

Racing shell
賽艇

Racing sloop
單桅小帆賽船

Supersonic car
超音速汽車

Racing yacht
賽艇

Dragon boat
龍舟

Coxless pair
雙人單槳無舵手艇

Coxless four
四人單槳無舵手艇

Powerboat
快艇

Superbike
超級摩托車

Track-racing motorbike
場地賽摩托車

Supermoto motorbike
滑胎摩托車

Motocross motorbike
越野摩托車

Dirt track racer motorbike
泥地摩托賽車

Grand Prix motorbike
格蘭披治摩托車

Speedway motorbike
沙地摩托車

Racing wheelchair
競賽輪椅

Cyclocross bicycle
公路越野自行車

Time-trial bicycle
計時賽自行車

Trials bicycle
攀爬自行車

Triathlon bicycle
三項鐵人自行車

Track bicycle
場地自行車

Rat rod
鼠桿賽車

Classic hot rod
經典鼠桿賽車

Kart
小型賽車

Off-road racing truck
非公路賽貨車

Midget racer
小型自行賽車

GT3
GT3 跑車

GT300
GT300 跑車

GT500
GT500 跑車

Rally car
拉力賽賽車

Touring car
房車

GP2 car
GP2 賽車

INDYCAR
印第賽車

Formula Ford car
福特方程式賽車

Formula 3 car
三級方程式賽車

Formula 1 car
一級方程式賽車

Racing sidecar
競賽側車

Racing truck
競賽卡車

Le Mans prototype
利曼原型車

Race safety car
競賽安全車

Stockcar
改裝賽車

Pro jet truck
噴射引擎卡車

Motorbikes 摩托車

Street bike
低規格摩托街車

Cruiser motorbike
摩托巡邏車

Streamliner motorcycle
流線型摩托車

Road superbike
公路超級摩托車

Universal Japanese motorcycle
通用日本摩托車

Electric motorbike
電動摩托車

Sport bike
運動型摩托車

Dual sport motorbike
雙重運動型摩托車

Bobber
改裝巡航摩托車

Rat bike
鼠形摩托車

Cabin motorcycle
包廂摩托車

Touring motorbike
旅行摩托車

Mini chopper
小型美式摩托車

Electric rocket drag bike
電動火箭直線競速賽摩托車

Motorcycle trike
摩托三輪車

Classic 1930s motorbike
三十年代經典摩托車

Derny
領跑摩托車

Chopper
美式摩托車

Feet first motorcycle
雙腳向前式摩托車

Café racer
咖啡館摩托車

Streetfighter bike
街頭霸王摩托車

Underbone
低骨架摩托車

Enduro motorbike
耐力越野摩托車

Sport touring bike
運動型旅行摩托車

Famous ships 著名的船

HMS Bounty
英國皇家海軍邦蒂艦

Cutty Sark
卡蒂薩克號

HMS Sovereign of the Seas
英國皇家海軍君權號

Golden Hind
金鹿號

Mary Celeste
瑪麗・賽勒斯特號

Bluenose
藍鼻子號

La Pinta
平塔號

Mayflower
五月花號

Nao Victoria
維多利亞號

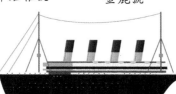
RMS Titanic
鐵達尼號

HMS Beagle
英國皇家海軍貝格爾號

SS Central America
中美洲號

Thermopylae
溫泉關號

Turbinia
渦輪號

Syracusia
敘拉古號

Great Republic
大共和國號

SS Savannah
薩凡納號

Historic ships 具歷史意義的船

Passenger steamship
載客蒸汽船

Tramp steamer
不定期貨運蒸汽船

Early oil-tanker
早期油輪

Palace steamer
宮殿蒸汽船

Snag boat
清障船

Steam yacht
蒸汽帆船

Hickman sea sled
克文高速摩托艇

Galleon
商用或軍用大帆船

Brig
雙桅橫帆船

Man-of-war
軍艦

Blackwall frigate
布萊克沃爾
巡防艦

Barque
三桅帆船

Fluyt
福祿特帆船

Screw barque
推進器三桅帆船

Baltimore clipper
巴爾的摩高速帆船

Panokseon
板屋船

Penteconter
古希臘槳帆戰艦

Dromond
高速大帆船

Quinquereme
古羅馬五段帆船

Bucentaur
中古威尼斯典禮船

Currach
獸皮船

Mtepe
縫合船

Turtle ship
龜船

Roman galley
羅馬槳帆船

Junk
中國式帆船

Galleass
加萊賽型戰船

Trireme
三列槳座戰船

Barquentine
前桅橫帆三桅船

Viking longship
維京長船

Roman merchant ship
羅馬商船

Egyptian papyrus boat
埃及紙莎草船

Cog
寇克船

Caravel
卡拉維爾帆船

Knarr
北歐單桅商船

Big ships 大型船艦

LNG tanker
液化天然氣載運船

Freight ferry
貨輪

Fast ferry
高速渡輪

Icebreaker
破冰船

Cross Channel ferry
英倫海峽渡輪

Great Lakes freighter
美加五湖貨輪

Aframax tanker
阿芙拉型油輪

Articulated tugbarge
鉸接式拖船

Crude oil tanker
原油油輪

Cable layer
布纜船

X-bow support ship
船頭倒置船

Flo-flo ship
特大重載船

Flettner's rotor ship
費萊拿旋轉船

Ro-pax ferry
載客滾裝船

Cargo liner
貨運商船

Chemical tanker
化學品船

Supertanker
超級油輪

Product tanker
成品油輪

Crane ship
起重船

Shuttle tanker
穿梭油輪

Trinity House tender
英國領港公會小船

Drillship
鑽井船

Tug
拖輪

Panamax ship
巴拿馬型船

Bulker
散貨船

Chain ferry
橫水渡

Pipe-laying ship
敷管船

Container ship
貨櫃船

Factory trawler
工廠拖網漁船

Platform supply vessel
石油平台補給船

Merchant vessel
商船

Suction dredger
吸挖泥船

Straight-decker
平甲板船

Heavy lift ship
重載船

Sailing boats 帆船

Bermudan sloop
百慕達縱帆船

Caïque
地中海小帆船

Bawley
漁船

Wayfarer dinghy
徒步旅行者小帆船

Trabaccolo
亞得里亞海雙桅帆船

Catboat
獨桅帆船

Trimaran
三體帆船

Wishbone ketch
鳥胸骨式牽索帆船

Yawl
高低桅小帆船

Tjotter
小漁帆艇

Tartane
單桅三角帆船

Ketch
雙桅小帆船

Schooner
雙桅縱帆船

Shad boat
北卡羅來納州
傳統漁船

Sharpie boat
美國平底漁船

Nordland boat
挪威西岸漁船

Topper
Topper 級別的
帆船

Cat-ketch
不設首帆雙桅
小帆船

Norfolk wherry
諾福克郡帆船

Sabot dinghy
單手小帆船

Drascombe Drifter
Drascombe 公司製造的
漂網漁船

Friendship sloop
友誼單桅船

Gundalow
美國東北部乾草船

Dhow
阿拉伯帆船

Felucca
三桅小帆船

Laser dinghy
激光級小帆船

Catamaran
雙體船

Skerrie skiff
平底小艇

Devon lugger
德文郡小帆船

Sydney Harbour skiff
悉尼港小帆船

In the water 水面或水底

Float tube
浮管

Bow rider
有舵小型快艇

Longtail boat
長尾船

Pirogue
獨木舟

Bass boat
貝斯船

Bathtub boat
浴缸船

Cuddy boat
休閒遊艇

Kayak
獨木舟

Waka
捕魚及渡河划艇

Slipper launch
木製泰晤士河艇

Flyak
水翼皮艇

Go-fast boat
快艇

Logboat
木船

Midget submarine
微型潛艇

Reed boat
蘆葦船

Deep-submergence vehicle
深潛船

Clyde puffer
燃煤單桅貨船

Raft
木筏

Sailing yacht
帆船

Bilibili
竹筏

Coble
平底小漁船

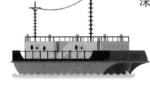
Lighter barge
平底貨運船

Shikara
印度西卡拉運輸船

Pontoon
蠆船

Tarai bune
盆型船

Masula boat
木製敞篷艇

Pump boat
泵船

Umiak
木框皮艇

Canoe
划艇

Pram boat
嬰兒船

Flatboat
平底船

Fishing boat
漁船

Supercavitation boat
超空穴效應船

Hydrofoil
水翼船

Houseboat
住家艇

Bathyscaphe
深海潛艇

Motor yacht
馬達遊艇

Jon boat
平底捕魚及狩獵船

Sampan
舢舨

Outrigger canoe
平衡體舟

Very Slender Vessel
高速穿浪船

Recreational submarine
遊樂潛艇

Coracle
獸皮小漁船

In the sky 天空

Tow plane
拖航飛機

Glider
滑翔機

Motor-glider
馬達滑翔機

Autogyro
自轉旋翼機

Double-blade
helicopter
雙槳直升機

Blimp
飛艇

Four-blade
helicopter
四槳直升機

Tilt rotor plane
傾轉旋翼機

Hot air
balloon
熱氣球

Tailless
glider
無尾滑翔機

Hopper
balloon
跳躍熱氣球

Unlimited
aerobatic
glider
自由特技滑翔機

Gas
balloon
氣體燃料氣球

Hang-
glider
滑翔翼

Rozière
balloon
混合燃料熱氣球

Flying boat
水上飛機

Biplane
雙翼機

Light-sport
aircraft
輕型運動飛機

Aerobatic
plane
特技飛機

Sky crane
空中起重機

Stunt
helicopter
特技直升機

Medium-lift
helicopter
中型運輸直升機

Zeppelin
齊柏林飛船

High-wing plane
機翼高置飛機

Primary glider
初級滑翔機

Twin-rotor helicopter
雙旋翼直升機

Gas turbine
helicopter
燃氣渦輪直升機

Homebuilt aircraft
自製飛機

Utility helicopter
通用直升機

Small propeller
plane
小型螺旋槳飛機

Pusher aircraft
推進式飛機

Low-wing plane
低翼飛機

Ultralight
helicopter
超輕型直升機

Light helicopter
輕型直升機

Microlight
微型飛機

Refuelling tanker
空中加油機

Fighter planes 戰鬥機

Shenyang
J-8 Finback

殲擊 8 型戰鬥機

Tejas Light
Combat Aircraft

光輝戰鬥機

Condor
bomber

禿鷹式轟炸機

Dassault
Mirage III

幻象 3 型戰鬥機

Fairey Swordfish
torpedo bomber

菲爾利劍魚式魚雷轟炸機

Dassault
Rafale C

C 型疾風戰鬥機

B-2 Spirit
'Stealth Bomber'

B-2 幽靈隱形轟炸機

P-61 Black
Widow

P-61 夜間戰鬥機

F-22
Raptor

F-22 猛禽戰鬥機

Gloster
Meteor

格羅斯特流星戰鬥機

F-35
Lightning II

F-35 閃電 II 式戰鬥機

MiG-15

米格 -15 戰
鬥機

P-51 Mustang

P-51 野馬式戰鬥機

P-40
Tomahawk

P-40 戰斧式戰鬥機

Junkers Ju-87
Stuka

Ju-87 俯衝轟炸機

F-18 Super
Hornet

F-18 超級大黃蜂
戰鬥攻擊機

Heinkel
bomber

亨克爾轟炸機

P-26
'Peashooter'

P-26 玩具槍戰鬥機

Sopwith Camel

索普維斯駱駝
戰鬥機

B-1 Lancer

B-1 槍騎兵戰略
轟炸機

Supermarine
Spitfire

噴火戰鬥機

Albatros D.III

信天翁 D III 型
戰鬥機

Fokker
Eindecker

福克 E 單翼戰鬥機

Hawker
Siddeley Harrier

霍克西德利鷂式
戰鬥機

Sukhoi
Su-30

Su-30 戰鬥機

Sea Harrier

海獵鷹戰鬥攻擊機

Hawker
Hurricane

颶風戰鬥機

Su-24 Fencer

Su-24 戰鬥轟炸機

F-16 Fighting
Falcon

F-16 戰隼戰鬥機

F-86 Sabre
jet

F-86 軍刀戰鬥機

Dornier Do-22
floatplane

多尼爾 22 水上飛機

Lancaster
bomber

蘭開斯特轟炸機

F-111
Aardvark

F-111 土豚戰鬥轟炸機

Mitsubishi
A6M Zero

零式艦上戰鬥機

F9F
Panther

F9F 黑豹戰鬥機

Vickers
Gunbus FB5

維克斯 FB5 戰鬥機

F4F
Wildcat

F4F 戰鬥機

SPAD S.XIII

斯帕德 XIII
戰鬥機

F-117
Nighthawk

F-117 夜鷹戰
鬥攻擊機

Eurofighter
Typhoon

颱風戰鬥機

F-14
Tomcat

F-14 雄貓式
戰鬥機

Su-37
Terminator

Su-37 終結者式
戰鬥機

SR-71
Blackbird

SR-71 黑鳥式
偵察機

SBD Dauntless
dive-bomber

SBD 無畏式俯衝轟炸機

MiG-23
Flogger

米格 -23
戰鬥機

F-4
Phantom

F-4 幽靈戰鬥機

F-15
Eagle

F-15 鷹式戰鬥機

Tanks and armoured vehicles 坦克及裝甲車

M2 Bradley
M2 布雷德利裝步戰車

Vector patrol vehicle
向量巡邏車

T-90
T-90 主力戰車

Mark I
Mark I 坦克

King Tiger
虎王戰車

Black Prince
黑王子步兵戰車

Churchill Crocodile
邱吉爾鱷魚坦克

Portee truck
機動炮車

Landing Vehicle
Tracked
履帶登陸車

Stryker mobile
gun system
史崔克機動火炮系統

Panther command
and liaison vehicle
黑豹指揮和聯絡車

M4
Sherman
M4 雪曼戰車

M113 armoured
personnel carrier
M113 裝甲運兵車

Churchill
邱吉爾戰車

Warrior armoured
vehicle
武士裝甲車

P40 Carro
Armato
P40 坦克

M3 half-track
M3 半履帶車

Sherman Crab
排雷車

M3 'Lee'
M3 李戰車

Challenger 1
挑戰者 1 式戰車

Fuchs armoured
personnel carrier
狐式輪型裝甲運兵車

Wolfhound patrol vehicle
獵狼犬巡邏車

Mastiff patrol vehicle
獒犬巡邏車

Warthog armoured
vehicle
疣豬裝甲車

Chieftain
bridgelayer
酋長式架橋車

Humvee
高機動性多用途
輪式車輛

Merkava Mk4
梅卡瓦 Mk4 主力戰車

Samaritan battlefield
ambulance
撒瑪利亞戰地救護車

Challenger 2
挑戰者 2 式戰車

'Little Willie'
小威利戰車

M728 combat
engineer vehicle
M728 戰鬥工程車

Challenger repair
and recovery vehicle
挑戰者維修及搶救車

Viking BVS10
BVS10 維京戰車

M1 Abrams
M1 艾布蘭主力戰車

Bren Gun
Carrier
布倫機槍運輸車

Battleships and submarines 戰艦及潛艇

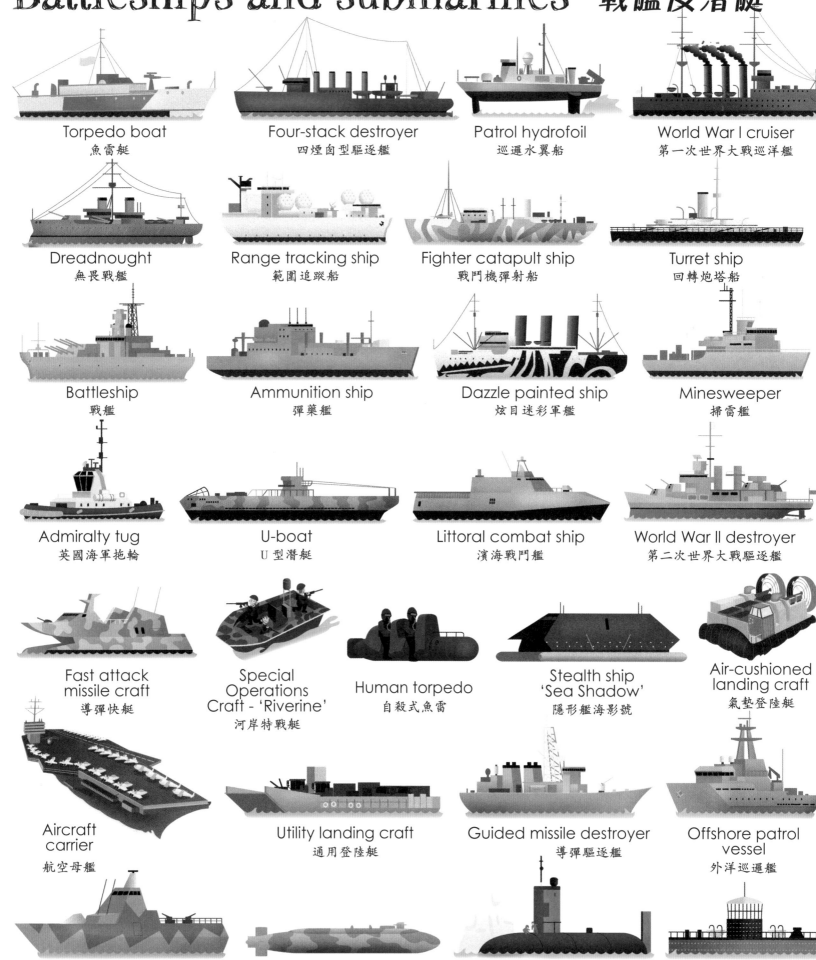

Torpedo boat
魚雷艇

Four-stack destroyer
四煙囪型驅逐艦

Patrol hydrofoil
巡邏水翼船

World War I cruiser
第一次世界大戰巡洋艦

Dreadnought
無畏戰艦

Range tracking ship
範圍追蹤船

Fighter catapult ship
戰鬥機彈射船

Turret ship
回轉炮塔船

Battleship
戰艦

Ammunition ship
彈藥艦

Dazzle painted ship
炫目迷彩軍艦

Minesweeper
掃雷艦

Admiralty tug
英國海軍拖輪

U-boat
U 型潛艇

Littoral combat ship
濱海戰鬥艦

World War II destroyer
第二次世界大戰驅逐艦

Fast attack
missile craft
導彈快艇

Special
Operations
Craft - 'Riverine'
河岸特戰艇

Human torpedo
自殺式魚雷

Stealth ship
'Sea Shadow'
隱形艦海影號

Air-cushioned
landing craft
氣墊登陸艇

Aircraft
carrier
航空母艦

Utility landing craft
通用登陸艇

Guided missile destroyer
導彈驅逐艦

Offshore patrol
vessel
外洋巡邏艦

Stealth corvette
隱形護衛艦

Ballistic missile submarine
彈道飛彈潛艦

Fleet submarine
艦隊潛艇

Monitor ship
淺水重炮艦

Military helicopters 軍用直升機

Mi-24 Hind
Mi-24 雌鹿

AH-1 Cobra
AH-1 眼鏡蛇

H-13 Sioux
H-13 蘇族

AH-64 Apache
AH-64 阿帕契

SH-3 Sea King
SH-3 海王

CH-54 Tarhe
CH-54 塔赫

UH-1 Iroquois
UH-1 休伊

Focke-Achgelis
Fa 223
Fa 223 龍式

Lynx Mk9A
Mk9A 山貓

MD 500 Defender
MD 500 防衛者式

SA-330 Puma
SA-330 美洲豹

H-34 Choctaw
H-34 喬克托族

UHT Tiger
UHT 型虎式

KA-27 Helix
卡莫夫 KA-27 蝸牛

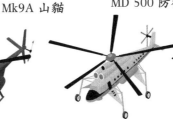
OH-6 Cayuse
OH-6 輕型印第安種小馬

Mi-10 Harke
Mi-10 重型運輸機

CH-47 Chinook
CH-47 契努克

UH-60 Black Hawk
UH-60 黑鷹

Diggers and excavators 掘進器及挖掘機

Trencher
掘溝機

Grader
平土機

Wheeled excavator
輪式挖掘機

Bucket wheel excavator
輪斗挖掘機

Tunnel boring
machine
掘進機

Roadheader
真空挖掘機

Suction excavator
輪式裝載機

Wheeled loader
吊鏈挖掘機

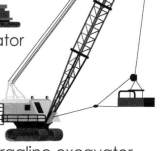
Dragline excavator
隧道挖掘機

Long reach
excavator
長臂挖掘機

Backhoe loader
挖掘裝載機

Giant loader
大型裝載機

Auger excavator
鑽地機

Tracked
excavator
履帶式挖掘機

Skid steer loader
滑移裝載機

Face-shovel
正鏟挖掘機

Site dumper
工地傾卸車

Grab excavator
抓斗式挖掘機

Mini excavator
小型挖掘機

Bulldozer
推土機

At the building site 建築工地

Concrete mixer truck
混凝土車

Builder's van
地盤貨車

Truck crane
起重卡車

Soil compactor
土壤壓實機

Self-loading
concrete mixer
自卸式混凝土車

Forwarder
木材吊運機

Double-
drum roller
雙輪壓路機

Boom truck
吊臂卡車

Forklift
truck
堆高機

Feller buncher
伐木歸堆機

Rigid dump truck
整體式自卸卡車

Piling rig
打樁機

Wheeled scrap
handler
輪式廢料
搬運機

Tracked scrap
handler
履帶式廢料
搬運機

Giant crane
大型起重機

Cherry
picker
伸縮臂升降台

Wrecker truck
拖吊車

Crawler crane
履帶式起重機

Pallet truck
托板車

Telescopic
handler
伸縮臂式叉車

Longwall
shearer
長壁採媒機

Asphalt
paver
瀝青攤鋪機

Swing yarder
擺式堆垛機

Track skidder
履帶式集木機

Ballast tamper
砸道機

Wheel tractor-
scraper
輪式拖拉鏟運機

Continuous miner
連續採礦機

Pipe layer
埋管機

Road planer
刨路機

Site supervisor
vehicle
工地主管車

Elevating scraper
升降式鏟運機

Low loader
低架式卡車

Articulated
dump truck
鉸接式自卸卡車

Yarder
堆垛機

Coal face
cutter
採掘面採煤機

Reclaimer
堆取料機

Concrete pump
truck
混凝土泵車

Trucks 貨車及卡車

Car transporter
車輛運輸車

Monster truck
怪獸卡車

Tipper truck
自卸卡車

Scissor lift truck
剪式升降台貨車

Lattice boom
truck crane
格子吊臂起重卡車

Delivery truck
運輸卡車

Rigid truck
整體式車架載重貨車

Catering truck
美食車

Container truck
貨櫃車

Curtainsider
側簾貨車

Mobile telescopic
crane truck
伸縮吊臂起重卡車

Milk tanker
牛奶運輸車

Logging truck
木材卡車

Highway
maintenance
truck
公路保養車

Big rig
半掛式卡車

Refuse collection
truck
垃圾車

Gully emptier
清渠車

Dekotora art
truck
日本暴走卡車

Heavy muscle
truck
重型肌肉卡車

Snow-clearing
truck
除雪車

Dropside
truck
農夫車

Dry bulk tanker
乾散貨槽車

Flatbed truck
平板卡車

Antenna transporter
天線運輸車

Mail truck
郵政車

Super-sized truck
超大型卡車

Tow truck
拖吊車

Panel truck
廂式車

Fuel tanker
油罐車

Pick-up truck
輕便客貨兩用車

Space Shuttle
transporter truck
穿梭機運輸車

Tractor-trailer
重型貨車

All-terrain truck
全地形卡車

Road-train
公路列車

On the farm 農場

Crop sprayer
農作物灑水車

Crop duster
農作物灑藥飛機

Disc harrow
圓盤耙

Livestock truck
牲畜運輸卡車

Loader wagon
裝運貨車

Horse van
運馬貨車

Manure spreader
施肥機

Farm trailer
農場拖車

Farm truck
農場卡車

Narrow tractor
窄軌距拖拉機

Giant tractor
大型拖拉機

Baler
乾草打包機

Six-wheeled tractor
六輪拖拉機

Hay tedder
乾草翻動機

Garden tractor
花園拖拉機

Forage harvester
青飼料收割機

Crawler tractor
履帶式拖拉機

Tool-carrier tractor
自動底盤拖拉機

Mini tractor
小型拖拉機

Post driver
豎桿機

Reversible tractor
雙向拖拉機

Out-front tractor mower
騎乘式割草機

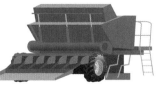
Potato planter
馬鈴薯種植機

Seed drill
播種機

Three-wheel tractor
三輪拖拉機

Harvester
收割機

Allen scythe
艾倫鐮刀割草機

Potato spinner
迴轉拋出型馬鈴薯挖掘機

Rubber track tractor
橡膠履帶式拖拉機

Swather
割草鋪條機

Front loader tractor
前置鏟斗拖拉機

Cultivator
耕耘機

Combine harvester
聯合收割機

Flail mower
連枷割草機

Root crop harvester
塊根農作物收割機

Sugar cane harvester
甘蔗收割機

Walking tractor
手扶拖拉機

Bean harvester
豆類收割機

High crop tractor
高處農作物拖拉機

Broadcast seeder
撒種機

Compact utility tractor
小型通用拖拉機

Grain cart
穀物運輸車

Cotton picker
採棉機

Old-fashioned things that go 舊式交通工具

Mail coach
郵件馬車

Clarence carriage
雙座四輪馬車

Brougham carriage
有篷四輪馬車

Surrey carriage
兩座四輪遊覽馬車

Conestoga wagon
科內斯托加式篷車

Coal box buggy
媒箱馬車

Prairie schooner
篷車

Dray wagon
平板貨運馬車

Farm wagon
農場四輪馬車

Landau carriage
雙排座四輪馬車

Chariot
雙輪馬戰車

Hansom cab
雙輪雙座馬車

Wagonette
四輪遊覽馬車

Concord stagecoach
康科德公共馬車

Hop tug wagon
短途四輪馬車

Dog cart
狗拉小車

Ellehammer helicopter
埃列哈默直升機

Bristol Boxkite
布里斯托箱形風箏

Wright Flyer III
萊特飛行器 III

Phillips Multiplane
菲利普斯多翼機

Berliner helicopter
貝利納直升機

Cornu helicopter
科爾尼直升機

Montgolfier balloon
孟戈菲氣球

Blanchard's balloon
布蘭查德氣球

Charles' hydrogen balloon
查理斯氫氣球

Lunardi balloon
侖那狄氣球

Penny-farthing
大小輪自行車

Hobby-horse bicycle
木馬自行車

Treadle bicycle
踏板自行車

Sail wagon
有帆四輪馬車

Buckboard car
引擎四輪木板車

Omnibus
公共汽車

Steam car
蒸汽車

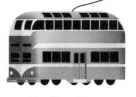
Trolleybus
無軌電車

Threshing machine
脫粒機

Daimler-Maybach motorcycle
粗製臨時摩托車

Roper steam motorcycle
羅柏蒸汽摩托車

Ploughing engine
犁田機

Steam tractor
蒸汽拖拉機

Steamroller
蒸汽壓路機

Steamshovel
蒸汽挖掘機

Steam locomotives 蒸汽火車頭

2-2-2 locomotive

2-2-2 火車頭

4-4-2 locomotive

4-4-2 火車頭

Fireless locomotive

無火火車頭

Articulated locomotive

鉸接式火車頭

Vertical boiler locomotive

直立式汽缸火車頭

Camelback locomotive

駱駝背火車頭

Duplex locomotive

複式火車頭

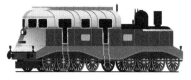

Heilmann steam-electric locomotive

希爾曼蒸汽電力火車頭

Rack-and-pinion locomotive

齒軌齒輪火車頭

Cab forward locomotive

駕駛室前置火車頭

Saddle tank locomotive

馬鞍油罐火車頭

Condensing steam locomotive

冷凝蒸汽火車頭

Fast goods locomotive

高速貨運火車頭

Geared steam locomotive

齒輪式蒸汽火車頭

Freight steam locomotive

蒸汽渦輪火車頭

Underground steam train

地下蒸汽火車頭

Electric-steam locomotive

電力蒸汽火車頭

'Tom Thumb'

湯姆拇指號

'Big Boy'

大男孩號

'Mallard'

野鴨號

'City of Truro'

特魯羅之城號

'John Bull'

約翰公牛號

'The Leviathan'

利維坦號

'Puffing Billy'

普芬比利號

'Stourbridge Lion'

斯托爾橋之獅號

'The Flying Scotsman'

飛翔的蘇格蘭人號

'The Kingston Flyer'

京士頓飛天號

'The Empire State Express'

帝國快車

'Adler'

鷹之號

'Fairy Queen Express'

精靈女王快車

Stephenson's 'Rocket'

史蒂芬森火箭號

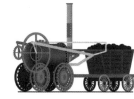

Trevithick's locomotive

特里維西克火車頭

Trains and trams 列車及電車

Monorail
單軌鐵路

Bullet train
子彈列車

Eurostar
歐洲之星

Class 370
Advanced
Passenger Train
先進客運列車 370 型

High-speed
train
高速鐵路

The Glacier
Express
冰河快車

Mail train
郵政列車

Cargo
tram
貨運電車

Class 180
passenger train
客運列車 180 型

Funicular
纜索鐵路

Miniature railway
微型鐵路

Express train
高速列車

Low-floor tram
超低底盤電車

Double-decker train
雙層列車

Rubber-tyred
Metro
膠輪路軌系統

Cane train
甘蔗列車

Maglev train
磁浮列車

Helper
locomotive
助推火車

Overhead train
高架電纜列車

Caboose
守車

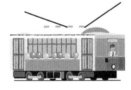
Trolley car
路面電車

Interurban
都市電車

Cog railway
齒軌鐵路

The Orient Express
東方快車

Mining train
採礦列車

Double-decker
tram
雙層電車

Gas tram
氣體燃料電車

Tram
engine
電車頭

Horse-drawn
tram
馬拉電車

Diesel train
柴油列車

Freight train
貨運列車

Tank wagon
罐車

Open wagon
敞車

Boxcar
棚車

Flatcar
平車

Pedalling, pushing and pulling 腳踏車、手推車及拖車

Banana board
香蕉板

Unicycle
單輪車

Gondola
貢多拉船

Recumbent bicycle
斜躺自行車

Conference bicycle
七人自行車

Lowrider bicycle
低底盤自行車

Child's tricycle
兒童三輪自行車

Skateboard
滑板

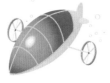
Human-powered submarine
人力潛艇

Trailer cycle
拖車自行車

Chopper-style bike
美式摩托型自行車

Freight bicycle
貨運自行車

Rowing boat
划艇

Handcycle
手踏車

BMX bicycle
極限自行車

Sculling boat
雙槳艇

Tandem
雙人自行車

Porteur bicycle
貨運自行車

Child trailer
兒童拖車

Pedibus
腳踏巴士

Space hopper
兒童跳跳球

Beach cruiser bicycle
沙灘休閒自行車

Orange-crate scooter
橙箱踏板車

Sociable bicycle
雙頭自行車

Small wheel bicycle
小輪自行車

Kick scooter
滑板車

Pogo stick
彈跳桿

Bicycle rickshaw
腳踏人力車

Dekochari art bicycle
日本暴走自行車

Longboard skateboard
長滑板

Wave board
柳葉滑板

Touring bicycle
觀光自行車

Velomobile
躺車

Wheelchair
輪椅

Quadricycle
四輪腳踏車

Hydro-bike
水上自行車

Human-powered aircraft
人力飛機

Micro scooter
小型踏板車

Handcar
臺車／手搖車

Mountain bicycle
山地自行車

Pedicar
腳踏四輪人力車

Punt
方頭平底船

Paddle skateboard
短槳滑板

Tricky terrain 奇特地形

4x4 pick-up truck
四驅卡車

Amfibidiver drivable submarine
水陸兩用潛艇

Hovercraft
氣墊船

Alligator amphibious tugboat
鱷式水陸兩用拖船

Sand yacht
陸上風帆

Amphicar
水陸兩用車

Beach buggy
沙灘車

Dog sled
狗雪橇

Dirt buggy
泥地越野沙灘車

Sledge
雪橇

Luge
仰臥滑行雪橇

Dune buggy
經典沙灘車

Float plane
水陸兩用飛機

Tundra buggy
冰原考察車

Duck tour bus
鴨子巴士

Seated sled board
坐式雪橇板

Sleigh
馬拉雪橇

Snowblower truck
除雪履帶車

Dirt bike
泥地越野摩托車

Snow plough
鏟雪機

Toboggan
長雪橇

Amfibus
水陸兩用巴士

Hydrocopter
滑水器

Swamp buggy
沼澤越野車

Hobbycar
水陸兩用車

Quad bike
四輪摩托車

All-terrain longboard
全地形長板

Sandmobile
沙灘摩托車

Snowmobile
摩托雪撬

Bobsleigh
有舵雪橇

Snow coach
雪上車

Screw-propelled vehicle
鑽地車

Snowplane
雪地飛機

Trail bicycle
林道自行車

All-terrain vehicle
全地形車

28

Rockets 火箭

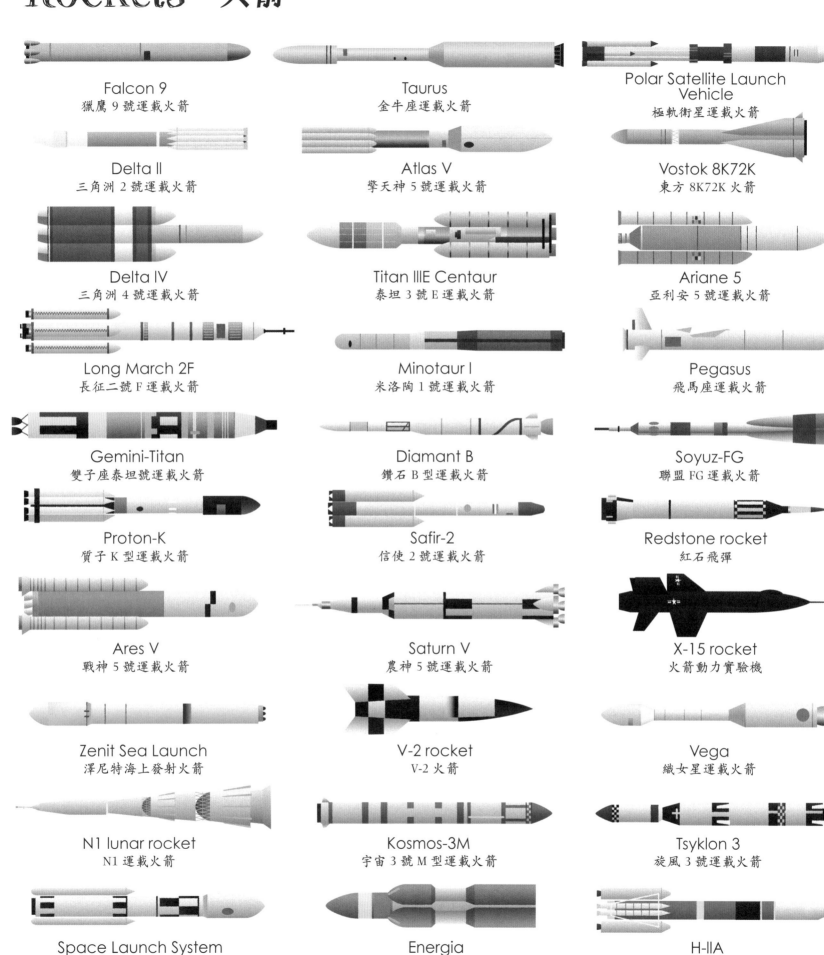

Falcon 9
獵鷹 9 號運載火箭

Taurus
金牛座運載火箭

Polar Satellite Launch Vehicle
極軌衛星運載火箭

Delta II
三角洲 2 號運載火箭

Atlas V
擎天神 5 號運載火箭

Vostok 8K72K
東方 8K72K 火箭

Delta IV
三角洲 4 號運載火箭

Titan IIIE Centaur
泰坦 3 號 E 運載火箭

Ariane 5
亞利安 5 號運載火箭

Long March 2F
長征二號 F 運載火箭

Minotaur I
米洛陶 1 號運載火箭

Pegasus
飛馬座運載火箭

Gemini-Titan
雙子座泰坦號運載火箭

Diamant B
鑽石 B 型運載火箭

Soyuz-FG
聯盟 FG 運載火箭

Proton-K
質子 K 型運載火箭

Safir-2
信使 2 號運載火箭

Redstone rocket
紅石飛彈

Ares V
戰神 5 號運載火箭

Saturn V
農神 5 號運載火箭

X-15 rocket
火箭動力實驗機

Zenit Sea Launch
澤尼特海上發射火箭

V-2 rocket
V-2 火箭

Vega
織女星運載火箭

N1 lunar rocket
N1 運載火箭

Kosmos-3M
宇宙 3 號 M 型運載火箭

Tsyklon 3
旋風 3 號運載火箭

Space Launch System
太空發射系統

Energia
能源運載火箭

H-IIA
H-IIA 運載火箭

In space 太空

Lunar Roving Vehicle
阿波羅月球車

Lunokhod rover
月球步行者

Venera-4
金星 4 號

Hubble Space Telescope
哈勃太空望遠鏡

Mir Space Station
和平號太空站

Kepler telescope
刻卜勒太空望遠鏡

Luna 16 probe
月球 16 號探測器

Sojourner rover
旅居者號

Mercury capsule
水星宇宙飛船

New Horizons probe
新視野號

Hayabusa probe
隼鳥號

Messenger probe
信使號

Opportunity rover
機會號火星漫遊車

Solar Dynamics Observatory
太陽動力學天文台

Galileo probe
伽利略號探測器

Vostok 1
東方 1 號

Columbia Command and Service Module
哥倫比亞號穿梭機

Salyut-7 Space Station
禮炮七號太空站

International Space Station
國際太空站

Phoenix Mars lander
鳳凰號火星探測器

Cassini probe
卡西尼號探測器

Helios probe
太陽神號探測器

Curiosity rover
好奇號火星探測車

Soyuz spacecraft
聯盟號宇宙飛船

Space Ship Two
太空船 2 號

Mars sky crane
火星探測漫遊者

Sputnik 1
史普尼克 1 號衛星

Sputnik 2
史普尼克 2 號衛星

Eagle lunar module
鷹號登月小艇

Voyager 1 probe
航行者 1 號探測器

White Knight Two
白色騎士 2 號

NASA Space Shuttle
美國航天總署穿梭機

Luna 1
月球 1 號

Viking 1 spacecraft
維京 1 號

Earth observation satellite
地球觀測衛星

Orbital test vehicle
軌道試驗飛行器

Unusual things that go 獨特工具

Quadrofoil
電動水翼船

Surface orbiter
船車混合動力器

Flying car
陸空兩用車

Sailing tanker
液貨船

Ekranoplan
翼地效應機

Tadpole trike
蝌蚪臥式三輪車

Camel bus
駱駝巴士

Transparent canoe-kayak
透明獨木舟

Gyrocar
單軌高架電動車

Circus wagon
馬戲團四輪大篷車

Sideways bicycle
側坐自行車

Ornithopter
撲翼機

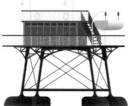
Sea-going tram
水上電車

Ice boat
冰上滑行水船

Backpack helicopter
背包式 直升機

Land Walker exoskeleton
"步行者"外骨骼 機械人

Howdah on elephant
象轎

Jet pack
噴射背包

Stunt plane
特技飛機

Sea tractor
拖拉機式水上車

Wood-powered El Camino
燃木埃爾卡密汽車

Electric diwheel
電動雙輪車

Monocycle
輪中單車

Volocopter
多軸直升機

Amphibious biplane
水陸兩用雙翼飛機

Paddlewheel canoe
腳踏艇

Six-wheeled car
六輪車

Powered street luge
電動街頭平底雪橇

Submersible watercraft
潛水船

Motorized monowheel
馬達輪中單車

Pocket bike
小型摩托車

Quadski
水陸兩用四驅車

Flying hovercraft
飛天氣墊船

Quadractor
森林拖拉機

Jetlev-flyer
水動力飛行背包

Zorbing ball
太空球

Slegoon
雪橇車

Stunt car
特技車

'Super Guppy'
"超級彩虹魚"運輸機

Alaskan land train
阿拉斯加陸上火車

Index 索引

1000 Things that Go
Copyright © 2015, 2018 Usborne Publishing Limited.
Chinese Mandarin (using complex characters) Translation
Copyright © 2019 The Commercial Press (H.K.) Ltd.

書名：兒童英漢詞彙大書——交通工具1000詞
作者：Rachel Wilkie and Hannah Wood
繪圖：Gabriele Antonini
出版：商務印書館（香港）有限公司
　　　香港筲箕灣耀興道3號東匯廣場8樓
　　　http://www.commercialpress.com.hk
發行：香港聯合書刊物流有限公司
　　　香港新界荃灣德士古道220-248號荃灣工業中心16樓
版次：2024 年 7 月第 1 版第 2 次印刷
©2019商務印書館（香港）有限公司
ISBN 978 962 07 0567 0
版權所有　不得翻印